Brooks

S

FIRE ON THE HILLS

FIRE ON THE HILLS

AND OTHER STORIES OF LONG AGO
Compiled by the Editors
of
Highlights for Children

Compilation copyright © 1995 by Highlights for Children, Inc.
Contents copyright by Highlights for Children, Inc.
Published by Highlights for Children, Inc.
P.O. Box 18201
Columbus, Ohio 43218-0201
Printed in the United States of America

All rights reserved

ISBN 0-87534-638-3

Highlights is a registered trademark of Highlights for Children, Inc.

CONTENTS

FIRE ON THE HILLS

By Joan Strauss

Ilse did not like anything about her new home in the brand-new state of Texas. How could her parents even call Fredericksburg a town? Even Willie and Hannah, her little brother and sister, loved this wild, rough place.

"Nothing but sod and log huts. Mud streets everywhere instead of gravel roads, too—even in this year of 1847!" Ilse thought out loud. "I wish we had stayed in Pennsylvania."

Although Ilse wouldn't admit it, she was scared.

She was frightened of the endless prairie, the wild windstorms, and the untamed animals. Most of all, Ilse was terrified of the Comanches.

It was almost Easter, but there would be no service in a church, no dinner at grandmother's, and no new holiday finery to wear.

The worst of it was Mama and Papa didn't seem to mind. "The wild game has been plentiful, and our crops will be good," her father said one morning at breakfast, "if the Comanches don't burn us out."

"Hush!" Her mother said, glancing nervously around the table. "I thought there was going to be a peace treaty with the Comanches." Ilse's stomach lurched with fear.

"John Meusebach has tried to make peace since we first arrived," her father replied. Ilse knew Mr. Meusebach was the leader of the settlers.

"The trouble is," her father continued, "some of the Mexican generals didn't want Texas to become part of the United States. They are urging the Comanche warriors to raid our settlements. The generals hope to drive us out and get Texas back as part of Mexico . . ."

He was interrupted by the sound of a horse's hooves clattering outside. A neighbor burst in the doorway. "Comanches on the warpath!" Mr. Taylor shouted. "Meusebach needs you, Weaver! We can stop the raids if Chief Kotemoczy and the other chiefs parley with us."

"Won't that be dangerous?" Ilse whispered, her eyes wide with fear.

"It's the only way," her father said. "They will not attack while we parley. Once they agree to a treaty, the settlers will be safe. Comanches keep their word." Ilse watched nervously as her father hurried to saddle his horse.

With the men gone, the women and children packed food, featherbeds, and other supplies and moved into the stockade for protection.

"It's not going to be much of an Easter shut up in this old fort," Willie grumbled that afternoon, as the children played inside the walls of the fort.

"Why don't those Comanches go home? Don't they want to get ready for Easter, too?" asked Hannah. She had stopped playing and was staring at the brown hills that overlooked the stockade.

Ilse laughed. "There are no Comanches here."

"Yes there are. Up there." Hannah pointed to the hills. Along the skyline stretched a row of warriors, unmoving atop their horses.

By now, others had seen them, too. Frightened as she was, Ilse remembered what her father had said: "Comanches keep their word."

"They won't attack," she assured Hannah and Willie.

The evening cooking fires inside the stockade were echoed by a ring of fires on the hills above. Were those the warriors' cooking fires, or were they lit for the wild war dances of the Comanches?

Mrs. Weaver was on guard duty, so Ilse put Willie and Hannah to bed. They were too excited by the day's happenings to go to sleep. Other children were fussing and crying, too. *Maybe they would be less scared if I told them a story,* Ilse thought.

Ilse cuddled her brother and sister close and called to the others. "When I saw the fires on the hills," she began, "I remembered that Easter is coming soon. It reminded me of an old, old story grandma told me.

"Long ago in Germany, when grandma was a young girl, people lit huge bonfires the night before Easter. Each village tried to have the biggest fire."

Looking around, Ilse noticed that many mothers had joined the circle. "The reason for the fires has been long forgotten," she continued. "The tradition goes back to ancient times when people were afraid the warm sunshine would not return after winter's ice and snow. They built the fires to coax the sun to come back."

She beckoned the children closer, as if to tell them a secret. "I think it was the Easter Bunny who built those fires on *our* hills," she said in a loud whisper. "He has to boil the dye to color lots of Easter eggs, now that so many children have come to Texas."

Willie and Hannah and the other smaller children forgot to be afraid. They went happily to bed to dream of the Easter Bunny.

Two mornings later, the line of warriors disappeared from the skyline. Soon after, riders galloped toward the stockade. Ilse felt her fear rise in her throat. But it was their own men, led by big John Meusebach on his big black horse.

He waved a paper over his head. "Chief Kotemoczy has signed a treaty! We are blessed with peace this Easter."

Once more in her father's arms, Ilse confessed how frightened she was.

"We were all worried," her mother said, "but Ilse put aside her own fear to calm the rest of us." She told how Ilse had quieted the children with her stories.

"The Comanches sent scouts to watch Fredericksburg during the parley," her father explained. "They built the fires to signal all was well. You were in no real danger, but I'm proud of your courage." He hugged her tightly. "You're a real prairie girl."

A week ago, Ilse would not have been pleased at this praise. But now, snuggled in the warm safety of her father's arms, Ilse began to think that Texas wasn't so bad, after all.

You Can Sell the Sun

By Beth Thompson

"Turnip man! Turnip man! Buy my turnips while you can!"

The street hawker's cry echoed in the cold morning air and floated up to the apartment above the street. Soon others joined it: "Fi-ish! Oh, fresh fi-ish!" "Milkman, ho! Mi-i-lk!" "Hot breads and muffins!"

"Boiled turnips taste good, Ma. Please put some in the soup you're making!" begged little Drucilla, tugging at her mother's patched brown skirt.

Mrs. Wilkins shook her head, smiling sadly at the tiny girl. Drucilla was too little to understand about money but not too little to feel hunger.

Thomas distracted his sister so she wouldn't make their mother feel worse about the watery, flavorless soup that would be their meal that night. "Look, Dru! I've made you a doll!" It was only a bit of straw with a scrap of colorful gingham tied on for a kerchief, but Drucilla beamed, no longer thinking about turnips. She immediately sat on the threadbare rug of the kitchen and hugged the doll. Thomas's ten-year-old stomach still grumbled with hunger as he listened to the hawkers' cries.

The truth was the Wilkinses were almost penniless now that Mrs. Wilkins had lost her housekeeping job; the family she worked for recently moved away. The cold September wind of 1833, whistling under the doorsill, reminded Thomas that winter was on its way to New York City, bringing new problems. Coal was expensive, so the family might have to choose between warmth for the body or food for the stomach.

"Car-rots! Peas-n-beans! Car-rots! Peas-n-beans!"

Remembering the thick stews his mother used to make, filled with potatoes and carrots, Thomas knew he must do something. They couldn't live on watery soup all winter.

"If we had a barrow, I could be a hawker, too," he said hopefully. "If we had something to sell."

"You can't sell *ifs,* boy," Mrs. Wilkins said sadly. She had that faraway look that meant she was thinking of Thomas and Dru's father, lost at sea a year ago. "Remember what your pa used to say," she said.

"You can't sell blue sky to a bird on the wing. And you can't sell the sun, so you might as well sing!" Thomas said in a rush.

The words brought back the memory of his father so keenly, Thomas had to blink back tears. Pa would have found a way, and so must he!

"Back soon, Ma," he said, struggling into his patched jacket as he opened the door.

Down in the crowded street, the bitter wind stung his bare hands, but a thin autumn sun shone down on the rumbling carts and hurrying people. John Stephenson's new-fangled invention, a horse-drawn trolley car, clanged as it stopped to pick up passengers. Last year, New York had only one trolley, but now there were many.

Thomas watched as a well-dressed man jumped from a bench and leaped aboard the waiting trolley. He'd left a pair of expensive tan gloves and a newspaper on the bench. Quick as a flash, Thomas snatched them up and raced to the trolley.

"Sir! Sir! You forgot these!" he cried.

The man took the gloves and smiled. "You keep the paper, son, and here, this is for your trouble!" He tossed a coin to Thomas as the trolley lumbered away, clanging its brass bells.

Thomas couldn't believe his luck. The dime in his hand felt as warm as a bit of the sun itself. There would be bread on the table after all! He stared at the smudged newsprint on the paper. It was a copy of the *New York Sun*, a new daily started just this month. Unlike the other papers, which cost 6¢ an issue, the *Sun* was priced at 1¢ to attract new readers. A large ad caught Thomas's eye:

NEWSBOY MERCHANTS WANTED—
Steady employment for enterprising boys willing to work hard selling the *Sun*. Vendors will receive a liberal discount. See Mr. Day at the *Sun* office.

Thomas was glad his mother had insisted he learn to read. He knew that a vendor was a salesman, but he wasn't sure what a "liberal discount" was. Pocketing his coin and tucking the paper under his arm, he set off to find out.

Mr. Day turned out to be 23-year-old Benjamin H. Day, the founder, editor, chief reporter, and typesetter of the *Sun*. He didn't look much older than Thomas himself, despite his handlebar mustache and fashionable clothing.

"I need boys willing to grab the public by the coattails, so to speak. They've got to be able to get 'em to buy the *Sun* instead of some other paper. Newsboys! It's my own idea!" Ben Day said proudly. "I sell you papers for 1/2¢ each and you resell 'em for a penny. You keep what you make, simple as that."

"I'll take 16 papers, sir," said Thomas without hesitation, handing over the coin.

"Ten cents will buy 20 papers, son," said Mr. Day. "Sure you want the rest in change?"

"Yes, sir. You see, if I'm no good at selling, at least I can take home a two-cent loaf of bread to Ma and Drucilla."

Ben Day grinned as he handed Thomas the papers and the change. "Oh, you'll sell the *Sun,* my lad. It almost sells itself! I know you can do it."

Funny, that's just what Pa had said to Thomas when he was struggling with the heavy coal bucket or frowning over his lessons, Thomas thought. So, with a smile and a whistle, Thomas set off to sell the *Sun* and surprise Ma and Dru with a real meal.

"Paper! Read all about it! New trolley line opens! Read all about it in the *Sun!* Paper! Penny a read! Buy the *Sun* for just one penny!" Thomas shouted, adding his voice to the busy song of the street hawkers.

FROZEN JOURNEY

By E. Jane Israel

Rebecca waited impatiently in the warm kitchen of her house on Swett's Pond Road in Orrington, Maine. It was a blustery, snowy afternoon in March 1850. She fidgeted with the tablecloth as she eyed the door to her parents' room. Papa had been in there with Mama for hours.

The door swung open, and she leaped to her feet. "Is Mama all right?" she exclaimed.

"She's failing," said Papa. "We must have a doctor." He shook his head slowly. "She birthed you with no trouble, but the midwife can't seem to help her this time. This baby just won't come. If only your cousin Tom had not gone to Castine yesterday. I could have sent him to Hampden for Doc Pritham."

Rebecca strode to her father and stood as straight and tall as her five foot, one inch frame would allow. "I can go, Papa," she said. "I know Mama needs you here. I can drive the team and sleigh as good as Tom."

"No, no," said Rebecca's father. "You're just a child. If only Hansen were still with us."

"I must go, Papa," said Rebecca. "There's no one else."

Papa sighed deeply. "You're right, daughter," he said. "I despair at the thought, but you must go."

"I will be fine, Papa." said Rebecca, already lacing up her boots.

"Wear your warm sweater under your coat," said her father.

"Yes, Papa."

"And your muffler."

"Yes, Papa."

"And your warmest hat and mittens," he continued with concern.

"Papa! I'll dress warmly," said Rebecca. "Please don't fret. I will be all right."

Joshua Lowell hugged his only daughter. "Go with God," he murmured. "I'll hitch the team to the sleigh."

Rebecca was on her way in fifteen minutes. *I'll be there soon,* she thought. *It's only eight miles.*

As the horses trotted through the snow, the wind picked up and snow began to fall. Rebecca hunched deeper into her coat and wished she could put her hands into a muff. She was grateful for the lap robe her father had tucked over her before she set out.

The storm worsened by the minute. Sugar and Honey were the best two-horse team around, but they were having difficulty. Occasionally they shook their heads and whinnied, as if to ask why they were out on such an afternoon. Rebecca prayed they would make it to the doctor's house before dark.

The swirling whiteness prevented Rebecca from seeing the trees along the roadside. She could no longer tell if she was still on the road.

Suddenly the sleigh lurched. Honey whinnied loudly and tried to rear as the sleigh slipped down an embankment. "Don't fall!" screamed Rebecca to the horses, her words lost to the wind. The sleigh tipped and landed on its side in a gulley, throwing Rebecca into the icy snow. Honey and Sugar struggled frantically to keep afoot.

Her eyes and mouth filled with snow, Rebecca groped her way to the sleigh and forced her frozen fingers to unhitch the team. Free of their burden, the horses stood still at the side of the gulley, quivering and snorting.

Rebecca struggled up the slope and stood a moment to catch her breath. Then she unharnessed the horses, leaving a soft bridle on each. She tapped the back of Honey's leg softly. "Down," she said. Honey lowered her front legs and Rebecca scrambled onto her. She wrapped Sugar's rein around her wrist. "Take me to Doc Pritham's," she said. "To the river, Honey."

They moved forward slowly. For hours the horses and Rebecca struggled, heads bent to the wind, plowing through the snow. Rebecca had no idea if they were going in the right direction; she could see no buildings in the blizzard. She prayed that Honey had understood her command to take her to the river crossing.

Exhausted and chilled, her hands and feet numb with cold, Rebecca nearly rode straight into the dock house at Mill Creek Crossing.

"Good girl, Honey!" she cried. She dismounted and went to the door of the tiny dock hut. It was locked tight. Her heart sank.

"If only Harkins was here with his sleigh, he

could take me across the river." said Rebecca to Honey. "Guess he's home snug and warm like most folks are on a day like this."

She then climbed onto Sugar and tied Honey's rein around her wrist. "Let's go, Sugar," she said. "Cross the river."

Daylight faded as they crossed the frozen expanse. Rebecca prayed that Sugar wouldn't slip on the slick surface hiding beneath the deep snow. The horses were tiring and they moved slowly, their hot breath freezing in tiny crystals on their noses.

Finally they reached the opposite shore. Doc Pritham's house was close to the river. Rebecca dismounted and walked the horses the last 100 feet. Still holding their reins, she pounded on Doc's front door. His chubby wife, Alice, opened it.

"We need Doc!" shouted Rebecca over the wind. Then she collapsed.

Rebecca awakened to see Alice Pritham standing by her bedside. Suddenly she realized her feet were no longer cold, and her toes touched the warm metal of Mrs. Pritham's brass bed warmer.

"Is Mama. . . ?" whispered Rebecca.

"Your mama is going to be fine," said Mrs. Pritham. "Doc just returned, and he brought a message for you from your papa."

"A message?"

"Yes, dear. He said to tell you that you have a brand-new baby brother."

"I do?" Rebecca said.

"And," continued Mrs. Pritham, "he says that this baby brother has some mighty big footsteps to follow in if he's going to be as fine and brave as his big sister."

Rebecca smiled and snuggled deeper under the comforter. "A baby brother," she murmured, then drifted back to sleep.

Secret Stitches

By Barbara Owen

The sun beat down on Louis as he raked the gravel yard of the little brown house. His calloused and sweaty hands pulled the rake through the gravel, smoothing it out. Pa usually did this job, but today he was working in the copper mine outside town.

"Hey, Louis, it's too hot for chores," called Pedro. "Let's go catch a burro and have a ride."

Louis smiled and leaned against the side of the house, surveying his work and the majestic

Arizona landscape beyond. "OK," he agreed, putting the rake in its ramshackle shed. The two hiked out toward the desert where the wild burros ran.

All morning the boys chased burros. They yelled, rode, and fell off, forgetting about the heat. When the sun was high, Louis remembered lunch. "I must get home and fix a meal for Pa," he told Pedro. "He'll be waiting for it at the store." He ran for home, filled a basket with biscuits, sausage, and a skin of cold water, then dashed toward town.

"You're late," said Pa, standing with some other miners at the back of the general store as Louis burst in. Suddenly the rough mining men started to laugh. Pa glanced around, frowning. Then Louis remembered what had happened when he fell off the burro that morning. Dropping the basket, he grabbed the seat of his pants.

The men laughed louder.

Louis turned red and hurriedly picked up the basket and set it on the counter.

"Riding burros again? In your good pants?" Pa spoke sternly.

"Yes, sir," Louis admitted, hanging his head.

"Did you finish raking?"

"No, sir. I . . . I'll take the pants to the seamstress," Louis sputtered. "Then I'll finish." He slipped out the door, as the laughter followed him.

Mrs. Wells, the town seamstress, eyed the pants Louis held out to her. "I'm very busy, Louis," she said apologetically. "I'm not taking any new work until after the Fourth of July."

"But I *have* to have my pants mended," Louis pleaded. "Pa is very angry."

"You boys should learn that riding wild burros is hard on the backside of your pants." Mrs. Wells scolded. "I'm sorry, Louis. I can't mend them now."

As Louis turned to leave, he noticed colorful fabric draped across a chair. "What a beautiful red and white quilt. Is that what you're sewing?" he asked.

Mrs. Wells stepped in front of her work as if trying to hide it. But it was much too large to be hidden. "You'll have to go now, Louis," she said.

"Couldn't you just show *me* how to fix the pants?" he asked.

She looked at the sorry condition of the pants he clutched in his hands. "Very well. Sit there. Take this needle and thread."

"Who is the quilt for?"

"Pay attention here." She showed him how to take tiny stitches. "You must sew exactly like this from here to there. Then let me see it."

Louis worked silently for a few minutes. Every time he looked up from his work, he saw Mrs. Wells carefully stitching another red stripe onto the huge quilt. At last Louis showed her his work. In an instant she ripped out all his stitches. "Take time. Do it well. Here. Again."

Louis sighed and threaded the needle again. *I wish I'd stayed home and raked gravel,* he thought. He began making the tiniest stitches yet. This time Mrs. Wells came over to watch.

"You're learning. These stitches will hold."

Louis smiled, pleased with his work. "When will you finish the quilt?" he asked.

"It is not a quilt, Louis. Can you keep a secret?"

"Yes, ma'am."

"It is a new flag to fly in the town square. It will be a surprise for the town."

"Will it have a star for Arizona, too?"

"Yes," said Mrs. Wells. "Our state became one of the United States on February 14 this year. Since a new star is added to the flag on the Fourth of July following admission to the Union, I decided to make the flag as a present for the town. But it has taken so much time that I'm behind with my paying work." Mrs. Wells sighed. "But I'm determined to finish the flag. The rest will have to wait."

"Could I help?" Louis stroked the beautiful new flag and felt the crisp cloth.

Mrs. Wells laughed. "You can sew up ripped pants right well, but you're not quite ready to work on a special flag." She looked at him seriously. "You could help me keep the surprise, though. Can you come tomorrow and the next day to mend some of the miners' shirts and pants? You could do that work, and I won't have to explain to everyone why I'm not getting my regular sewing done."

During the next two days Louis sewed and sewed. He had callouses on his fingers from holding the needle, but the customers were pleased with their mended clothes. No one guessed about the town surprise.

"How will you present the flag?" asked Louis a few days later. He sat cross-legged on the floor, finishing a new seam on a shirt.

"I am hoping to switch it for the regular flag. Then when it's hoisted up, everyone will see the new stars."

"Hey, I could switch it for you," Louis said excitedly. "The regular flag is kept in the store. I can put this one in place of the old one when I take Pa his lunch."

At dawn, on the Fourth of July, 1912, everyone in the little Arizona town gathered in the courthouse square.

Pedro's father played the bugle. Louis's father was given the honor of attaching the flag to the rope on the flagpole. Louis stood by to help.

"Someone must have cleaned the flag," Pa whispered. "It looks so bright." Louis just smiled.

Up it went. The crowd watched, all knowing that this was their first Independence Day as a new state. Then someone noticed. "It's a new flag! Look, forty-eight stars."

People began counting. "Sure enough, there's forty-eight!"

Soon the story was out. People thanked Mrs. Wells, and she told how Louis helped her. Pa looked surprised, then proud. He put his hand on Louis's shoulder. "Perhaps someday you will be a fine tailor," he said.

"And I won't have to worry when I ride wild burros because I can always mend my pants if they need it!" Louis exclaimed.

Pa just laughed.

Harriet's Promise

By Marilyn Kratz

Harriet smiled as she climbed the ladder to the loft in the small sod house. Her little sisters, Kate and Amanda, were napping, Pa was in town, and James was out checking his traps. She had the rest of the afternoon to herself.

Harriet opened the small box in the corner of the loft. Carefully, she lifted out her precious books.

She ran her fingers over the red velvet cover on the smallest book and remembered the evenings, long ago, when Ma had read poems from it as they sat around the stove. That was her favorite memory of Ma.

She glanced at the pictures in a thin book of Bible stories and laid it aside.

Harriet's favorite book was the one bound in a stiff black cover. The name *Harriet* was on the cover because someone named Harriet had written it. Inside were pictures Harriet could look at for hours, even though she didn't quite understand them.

Why is that pretty lady carrying her child across that icy river, she wondered. And why is that old man so sad?

Someday, she promised herself, I will learn to read. Then I will know the answers.

The opening of the door suddenly interrupted her daydreams.

"I heard in town that a teacher has been hired for our school, James," Pa was saying, as he and James entered together. "The term begins next week, and you will go."

Harriet scrambled down the ladder. "Oh, Pa! May I go to school, too?"

"I'm sorry, Daughter," said Pa. "I need you here to look after the girls. Besides, it's more important for James to go. A man needs an education."

Harriet blinked back the tears that sprang to her

eyes. She wanted to scream, It's just not fair! I want to learn, too!

She swallowed the words along with the lump which had risen in her throat, but she did not forget the promise she had made that afternoon.

Harriet thought of nothing else during the rest of that week. Monday morning, as she packed a lunch for James, she told him of a plan she had made.

"James, you must listen carefully and study hard," she said. "Every day, when you get home, I want you to teach me everything you have learned."

"I don't even want to go to school," James grumbled.

"Oh, James! Don't you know how lucky you are!" cried Harriet. "You can learn to read. My only chance to learn is through you. Please try, for both of us!"

Each afternoon, Harriet waited anxiously for James to come home from school. She made him sit right down and go over the day's lessons with her. But, on Thursday afternoon, James slammed the books on the table.

"It takes too much time to teach you everything," he complained. "I haven't checked my traps for three days, and I still have my chores to do."

"I'll help you," Harriet said quickly. "I'll do all your chores while you are in school, I promise."

"Even feeding the sow?" he asked suspiciously.

Harriet swallowed. She was afraid of the huge sow, especially now that she had a litter of piglets. But she answered, "Even the sow."

"Done!" James said, as he left to check his traps.

The next day, as soon as Harriet's little sisters were napping, she hurried out to do James's chores. As she milked the cow and carried in corncobs for the stove, she tried to recall everything James had taught her about letters and numbers.

Finally, it was time to feed the sow. Harriet could feel a knot form in her stomach.

She slowly filled a bucket with corn and carried it to the sod pig shed. She cautiously opened the door. The sow lay sleeping in the middle of the floor, her piglets surrounding her. Harriet breathed a quiet sigh of relief.

Then she saw the sow's trough in a corner of the little shed. How could she ever get around that huge animal without waking her? Harriet wondered.

Harriet thought about pouring the corn on the floor and hurrying away. But she knew how hard Pa had worked to harvest every kernel. *That won't do,* she thought.

Taking a deep breath, Harriet inched her way noiselessly around the sleeping sow. She tried to pour the corn into the trough very quietly. But at the sound of the first kernels dropping, the sow gave a loud snort and scrambled to her feet.

The bucket clattered into the trough as Harriet sprang to the top of an old barrel in the corner. Her heart seemed to be pounding in her head.

The sow stood below her, blocking the way to the door. Her small eyes glinted up at Harriet as she grunted and snapped her teeth.

Harriet opened her mouth to shoo the sow away, but only a sob came out.

Grunting, the sow climbed onto the side of the barrel with her front hooves. Her huge, biting mouth came closer to Harriet's feet.

Suddenly, there was a shadow in the doorway. Pa burst into the shed.

"Run, Harriet!" he shouted, forcing the sow back with a shovel.

Harriet jumped down from the barrel and dashed out of the shed. Pa hurried out after her and pulled the door shut.

"Are you hurt, Daughter?" Pa asked.

Harriet could only shake her head.

"What were you doing in there?" demanded Pa.

It took a minute for Harriet to catch her breath. Then she told Pa about her bargain with James.

When she was finished, Pa grew quiet. "Does learning to read mean so much to you?" he asked.

"Oh, yes, Pa," said Harriet. "I must learn to read. There must be a way—" She stopped, her eyes shining with unshed tears.

Pa rubbed his chin and looked at Harriet. Then he smiled. "We will find a way, Daughter," he said. "I reckon your grandma would help out with the girls for a few weeks while school is in session. I'll see about it tomorrow, I promise."

Tomorrow—I promise—the words echoed in Harriet's heart like a song, and no song had ever sounded better.

How Seth Becomes a Hero

By Philip Brady

"Remember, Mistress Bagley, don't let those two rascals inside your cabin," Sheriff Gale called over his shoulder, as he spurred away from the cabin. "Don't give them any food. They are dangerous men. I do wish your John was here."

The words kept echoing through Seth's mind as he split the last few chunks of firewood his father had cut before leaving for Concord. Sheriff Gale had called the warning two days ago as he raced to alert their neighbor, Abel Straw, a mile away on Badger Hill.

Seth's worried blue eyes uneasily raked the tiny, lonely clearing and the surrounding forest for the hundredth time. Nothing. An early snowfall had turned the ground a dusty white, and the woods were silent. Even the crows on the tall pines across the river had stopped their cawing.

It was that silence that made him uneasy. It had been three weeks since his father slid his big canoe into the nearby Pemigewasset, loaded his catch of furs, and started down river. Seth knew that even if his father sold all his pelts the first day, he wouldn't be back for at least another week.

"One is tall and thin," Seth had heard the sheriff say to his mother. "He's got a cocked eye. The other is shorter and limps a bit. They deserted our New Hampshire troops at Fort Ti. Don't be fooled by any sweet talk, mistress. They have been chased mighty hard and are hungry and desperate."

Seth's thoughts were interrupted as six-year-old Hannah darted out the cabin door. "Wood," she called, laughing gleefully, "piece of wood, Seth."

It was a game they played. Hannah was too little to carry more than a single stick, but she loved to help him. He carefully placed one piece into her chubby arms and followed her into the cabin, dumping his armful of kindling into the woodbox, next to the fireplace.

The mouth-watering smell of squirrel stew followed him outside, and his stomach rumbled. He'd been splitting wood all morning. Between the exercise and the cold air he'd honed a sharp edge on his hunger.

All the wood chunks his father had chopped were now split. To keep the fire going, he'd have to split some of the smaller logs lengthwise, then saw them into chunks. He didn't have the strength to saw the bigger logs.

Seth cast a wary eye about the clearing. Nothing stirred. Seizing a small limb, he pried a long elm log away from the pile his father had dragged in from the fell piece.

Dropping his pry pole, Seth picked up their single metal wedge. It was small, but his father had shown him how to start a good center crack, then switch to a thicker wooden wedge.

He placed the wedge close to the log's end and swung three hard blows with the wooden maul. With a loud snap a wide crack snaked along the log, then hung, blocked by a gnarled spot where a limb had grown.

Seth groaned and shook his head disgustedly. His father could drive the wedge out of sight with one blow, but Seth didn't have the heft to hit the wedge very hard. Straightening, he looked about for a wooden helper wedge—then froze. His heart started thumping so hard he felt sick. Not twenty feet away, two rag-tag men stood watching him. The tallest smiled, showing a mouth of broken, tobacco-stained teeth.

"Didn't go to startle you, lad. Snow kills sound, I guess." The voice was friendly, but the blood-shot brown eyes were like ice. "Could we get a mite of grub?"

Seth's hands tightened on the maul's handle. He glanced quickly toward the cabin. Thankfully, his mother hadn't heard.

"Is squirrel stew all right?" he asked, forming his mouth into what he hoped looked like a smile. *Please, Lord,* he prayed silently, *don't let Hannah come running out.*

The man's eyes darted about the clearing. "You alone, lad?" It was casually said, but the dirty hands tensed around a musket the man held.

Seth drew a deep breath. "No, Mother and Hannah are fixing our nooning. Squirrel stew, hot corn bread, and mulled cider. You're welcome to noon with us."

The men exchanged glances, relaxed.

Seth kicked the log with his foot. "Would you grab the crack and pull toward you, hard? I don't have the strength to do it." With a mighty effort he kept his voice steady, friendly. "Vittles should be ready in a few minutes." He held his breath.

The tall man propped his gun against the log pile. His companion hesitated, then did likewise. They dropped to their knees, side by side, four grimy hands grasping the log.

"Give the wedge one good whack, lad. Pull hard, Jake."

Seth swung the maul. His aim was true. The wedge flew sideways, out onto the frozen ground. Both men yelled as the log snapped shut, holding their fingers fast.

"I've got them! I've got them!" Seth yelled. He threw himself into his mother's arms as she ran across the yard. The two men's yells turned to angry shouts as they realized they were trapped. Quickly his mother grabbed the guns and stepped away from the two men.

"It's just what happened to my hand last year. It didn't hurt, but boy, I was stuck tight. Dad got me free. Remember?" He fought back the hot tears that were beginning to burn his eyes.

"Watch them close, Mother," Seth called as he made for the forest road. "I'll run fetch Mr. Straw."

Danger
on the
Underground

By Kathy Millhoff

"Won't this churning never be done?" complained Rose with a sigh.

"Ever," Melda said in that missy-prissy voice of hers. "You should say, 'Will not this churning ever be done?'"

Rose ignored her older sister and churned the butter more furiously.

Melda was washing and boxing the last of the eggs. It had been Melda's idea to make some extra money by selling butter and eggs. Pa had agreed but said, "You two handle it. I've got all I can do to farm this place. Mind, you don't neglect your other chores."

Rose thought about those chores now: chickens to feed, eggs to collect and sort, cows to milk, and butter to churn. Then there were their household chores, too: cleaning, washing, cooking, and preserving. Was it any wonder that, after their mother's death last spring, there had been no more time for school?

Rose let the churn paddle flop. "We don't have any fun any more."

"I suppose," Melda sighed, "that a child of eleven is bothered by such things. At my age we've given up such notions." Rose hated it when Melda acted grown up, when anyone could see that, at thirteen, her hair was still in braids.

A clatter of hooves and cart wheels interrupted the talk. Melda went to the door, and Rose heard her call, "Morning, Dr. Kyle."

"Morning, Miss Melda. Your pa at home?"

"He's out getting in the corn. Won't you come in?"

"I'll just leave this letter for him, thanks. See he gets it?"

"We will, Dr. Kyle," Rose said.

"He's been leaving lots of letters for Pa this year," Melda mused. "I wonder if it's got anything to do with the talk of war and free states."

"What's all this talk of war on such a fine day?" Pa's voice came from the door.

The girls jumped, startled by his sudden presence. Then Melda handed him the letter.

Pa's face hardened as he read the letter. When he finished, he crumpled it and dropped it into the stove.

Then, turning to the girls, he said, "Rose, pack up a hamper—chicken, bread, butter, pickles, and whatever's left of the pie. Melda, you bundle up some of Sarah's old clothes."

Rose was startled each time she heard her mother's name. Pa never said "your mother" or "your ma"—always "Sarah."

"What is it, Pa?" Melda asked.

"Girl, when you're meant to know a thing, I'll tell you. This butter and egg business will have to wait." He left for the barn.

"It *is* war," Rose whispered.

"Stop," Melda snapped, but Rose could hear her teeth chattering.

When everything was packed, Pa drove the team to the door. To Melda he said, "Stay home today and get all the chores done. If anyone comes by to ask, I've taken Rose to Cincinnati to the doctor."

Hiding her surprise, Rose slipped off her checked apron, grabbed her cloak and bonnet, and climbed into the wagon as Pa started the team.

Out on the road, high on the wagon seat, Pa began talking.

"Rosie, everyone hereabouts knows Sarah and I talked to doctors about you, trying to get some help. No one will wonder about us making a trip to the city."

Rose knew that no doctor could help her eyes see again. It wasn't something she thought much about. But now Pa was saying they were pretending. Why?

"We'll be fetching a girl, Celia Dillard, and taking her to the Morrisons," Pa continued.

Rose remembered the Morrisons, a Quaker family. She loved listening to their stories.

"We must continue to change the wagons and homes these people use," Pa went on. "Celia's going to Canada. Do you understand?"

"No, sir." Rose didn't understand anything.

"She's a slave, child. People are secretly helping her escape north to Canada. We'll help her from Cincinnati to the Morrisons."

"How, sir?"

"You'll sit on the bundles covering her. Anyone stops us, you let me talk."

"And us, sir?" Rose croaked. Suddenly she felt cold. She wanted to be running home, back to the horrible churning and to bossy Melda.

Pa didn't answer. Rose knew that the punishment for helping runaway slaves was very bad.

They rode in silence. Rose began to remember the night sounds of creaking wagons and whispers that had awakened her lately. She remembered the talk of slaves running north to freedom. She had never thought it had anything to do with her. That was all changed now that she was helping Pa.

Cincinnati was three hours' drive from the farm. By the time they reached the wharves on the river, Rose was glad to stretch her legs.

She knew that Celia Dillard was taken from a cotton bale on the wharf and hidden inside the bundles under the wagon seat. She suspected that people hadn't noticed it because, as usual, they were too curious about the doings of a blind girl. She could only hope they hadn't noticed.

When they were away from the wharves, Pa said, "It's about two hours to the Morrisons, then four more back to our place. Let's have some of chicken."

Pa sounded so cheery. Wasn't he scared?

Then she thought about Celia. She must be terrified. Probably hungry, too.

"Can't take a chance. Someone might see—"

As his voice trailed off, Rose heard the horses coming fast behind them. *Three or four,* she thought.

"Keep still," Pa whispered, as he drove to the roadside and stopped.

"Mister," called out one of the men, "dark coming on."

"We're headed home," Pa said quietly.

"I'm the deputy sheriff hereabouts," the man said. "We're tracking down some runaway slaves. There's a reward for them in Kentucky."

"I've seen no one," Pa began.

"No?" the deputy cut in. "We're checking all northbound wagons."

"I've had my daughter to a doc in Cincinnati," Pa explained. "As you see, she's blind."

"Sorry, Mister, but we're checking everyone."

If they'd packed her in the icehouse, Rose couldn't have felt colder than at that moment. Now they would know Pa had broken the law.

Then she heard someone screaming, "Pa! Pa! It hurts! I've got to get to my medicine! Please!"

She couldn't believe this. What was making her take on so? She'd never had medicine for her eyes, and she'd never felt any pain from them at all.

"Go on, Mister," the deputy was shouting, "help your girl."

After the men had ridden over the hill, Rose heard an odd sound. Then she realized—Pa was laughing! He rocked with laughter. He hadn't laughed so in years.

"Who would have thought I had such a little actress? I'm sorry we can't tell this to the Morrisons, but the more we keep things secret, the better for all." Rose began to smile a little, too, and soon they were both chuckling and talking.

After Celia was safely delivered to the Morrisons, Rose began to relax. Home was waiting, and so were Melda and the churning.

THE CUCKOO IN THE COVERED WAGON

By Bonnie Highsmith Taylor

Travis helped his father unyoke the oxen and turn them out to graze. "Why are we making camp in the middle of the day, Pa?" Travis asked.

"The group needs to do some washing and baking," Pa answered. "Some harnesses need mending, and a few of the wagon wheels need greasing. We'll camp here by the river until morning."

Great! thought Travis. He had been looking forward to fishing and swimming with the other boys in the wagon train. He ducked behind his family's wagon and started off when a voice called, "Travis!"

It was Ma, of course. He thought about pretending not to hear, but he knew it was no use. Reluctantly he turned back.

"Travis!" Ma repeated. "If you're through helping your Pa, get Granny's things down out of the wagon and set them up."

"Aw, Ma," Travis groaned.

"Never mind now," said Ma. "Granny is old, and it's not been easy making such a move at her age. If it gives her comfort . . ."

"But, Ma, it's such a nuisance hauling all that junk out every time we stop."

Ma smiled and patted his shoulder. "I know, dear, but it makes the trip easier for her."

Grumbling, Travis untied the heavy oak rocker from the back of the wagon and set it on the ground under a tree near the wagons. "There you are, Granny," he called.

Granny hobbled over and lowered herself down into the rocker. She leaned back, closed her eyes, and smiled. "Ah," she sighed. "Almost like being back home again."

Travis climbed into the wagon and got Granny's tea tray out. He unfolded the legs on the little tray and set it next to Granny's chair. On the tray he placed her china tea set and velvet-covered photo album. Then he handed Granny her parchment fan.

As Granny fanned herself and rocked back and forth, Travis started to tiptoe away. But Granny's voice stopped him in his tracks. "Just where do you think you're going, young man? Get my clock this minute."

Travis moaned. This was the part he hated the most. At every stop Granny insisted that her genuine hand-carved cuckoo clock, the one her papa had brought all the way from the old country, be hung. Travis was glad the train had stopped so close to a tree.

Granny reached into her apron pocket and pulled out her hankie. Slowly she unwrapped a large nail—the same nail that Travis had used on the entire trip. He took the nail and pounded it into the tree with a rock. He hung the clock and pulled down the chain that wound it.

Travis was very fond of his grandmother but this always embarrassed him. He didn't mind the rocking chair so much. Even setting up the tray and the tea set wasn't that bad, even though it was silly and a lot of trouble. Hanging up that cuckoo clock out in the middle of nowhere made him feel downright foolish.

What was worse, the other boys teased him about it. Like right now. Billy and Matt Baldwin, from the next wagon, were gathering firewood. As they passed by Travis they called, "Cuckoo! Cuckoo!" then ran off laughing.

"Dinnertime," Ma called. "Come and get it."

Travis didn't hesitate a minute. He was starved. He handed Granny a plate then gulped down his salt pork and corn bread and molasses.

After dinner, Pa went off to help Ma carry a load of wash to the river. Travis gathered the plates, knives, and spoons and dumped them into a kettle of hot water hanging above the fire.

Just then he heard a snuffling, grunting sound behind him. When he turned around, he saw a big brown shaggy bear lumbering into the camp. Travis's voice froze in his throat as the animal walked within six feet of him and gobbled up the last piece of corn bread in Ma's baking pan. With a giant paw it swatted the coffeepot through the air.

Travis tried to yell, but nothing came out.

As the old bear walked upright with one paw outstretched toward the cuckoo clock, Travis shot a glance at his grandmother. Please, Granny, he pleaded silently, don't do anything. Never mind that old clock.

But Granny wasn't about to sit by and do nothing

when her precious heirloom was in danger. Just as the old lady yelled, "Don't you touch that clock, you mangy critter!" the clock struck noon. Chimes rang out, and the cuckoo bird flew out of the little door. The bear was so startled that it flew backward, tripped over Granny's feet, and went sprawling on the ground.

Granny whacked it across the nose with her fan. With a deep rumbling roar, it scrambled to its feet and kicked up dust as it tore out of the camp.

By the time the twelfth cuckoo had sounded, there wasn't hide nor hair of that old bear anywhere in camp.

Ma and Pa ran to Granny's side. "Are you all right?" they both cried at once.

Granny laughed. "I'm fine. And that's a lot more than I can say for that shaggy beast."

Travis put his arm around his grandmother's shoulder and said, "Granny, I promise I'll never complain about your cuckoo clock again as long as I live."

The Hobos

By Helen Kronberg

Nina drove the cows home from pasture, lazily swinging a willow switch to keep them from wandering off the road.

As the cows lumbered over the railroad tracks near home, Nina noticed three men sitting on the ground beside the tracks. *They'll be at the house soon,* she thought. Hardly a week went by that a hobo didn't come to her house looking for a meal.

Mama didn't let them come in the house, though. "The way they live, they might have lice," Mama often said. But she was generous with food, and anyone who came was served on the back porch. Sometimes a hobo even slept in the barn for a night before moving on.

As Nina crossed the tracks, she heard the men talking. She gasped. *What language is that?* she thought. She glanced back after she'd passed. She was relieved to see they hadn't moved. Nina urged the cattle on, but they had their own infuriatingly slow pace. She tried not to look back.

As soon as the cows were in the barnyard, Nina rushed into the house. "Mama, there are hobos on the railroad tracks. Three of them."

Her mother laughed. "So start making sandwiches. Slice the meat thick. They're always hungry as bears."

Nina's hands shook. The knife clattered against the table.

"For goodness sake, Nina! What's gotten into you?" Mama said. "One would think you had never seen a hobo before."

"These are different," Nina said. "I heard them talking. They sounded real strange."

Her mother chuckled. "Are you sure they weren't some of our Norwegian neighbors?"

Nina shook her head. "I know what Norwegian sounds like. Besides, only the old people speak Norwegian. These men aren't old."

Mama shrugged. "Hand me the knife. You're in no shape to slice meat."

Silently they piled a plate with sandwiches. Soon they heard a knock at the door. Even though she had been expecting it, Nina jumped.

A man stood at the door, and two others stood a little apart behind him. The hobo pointed to his friends, then at himself. "Albert, Carl, Hans," he said. "Vork? Vork good."

Mama shook her head. "No work. But there's food." She motioned for Nina to bring the plate of sandwiches.

"Hungry, yes," the man said. "Must vork!"

Mama sighed and placed the sandwiches in the icebox to keep cool. "Get your papa, Nina. Maybe he can give them something to do."

When Nina returned with her father, Hans rose and came toward them. "Vork?" he asked.

Papa looked at the men. "Have you done farm work?"

Hans nodded. "From boy, vork farm."

"Where?"

"Vork farm, Germany. Vork sometimes, then no more. So we come America last year 1919."

Nina gasped and moved closer to her mother. "German," she whispered. "They're Germans."

"Hush," said Mama. But Nina felt her stiffen.

Nina felt gooseflesh rise on her arms, remembering all those graves in the cemetery on the hill. Graves of the young soldiers killed fighting The Great War with the Germans. No wonder she had been afraid!

Nobody spoke for a long time. Slowly Dad seemed to relax. "I'll put it to you plain," he finally said. "It won't be easy for a German to find work. Not around here."

Hans nodded, but a stubborn look clouded his eyes. "Vork hard. Sometime make home."

Papa rubbed his chin. "I've got a few odd jobs you can do today. Tonight you can sleep in the barn. In the morning we'll give you a good breakfast. Come."

He put Albert to work splitting wood for the cook stove. Carl hoed the garden. Hans followed Papa to the barn. Nina followed behind, watching from afar. When Papa emerged from the barn alone, Nina fled to the house.

At suppertime, Papa took buckets of hot water to the porch. The men rolled up their sleeves and scrubbed. They loosened their collars and washed as far as they could. They even soaped and scrubbed their heads. Then Papa brought them into the kitchen. Nina was shocked as they took seats at the table with the family.

Nina kept sneaking peeks at them, but she was careful never to look at their faces. She felt as if something terrible would happen if they looked directly into her eyes.

After supper, as Mama and Nina washed dishes, all three visitors went to the barn with Papa. Then Mama lit the kerosene lamp and sat down to darn socks.

"Everything all right?" she asked as Papa came in.

He nodded. "I get the feeling it's the best they've had for a long time. They're grateful." He sat down and began mending a broken bridle. "I sure could use some help this summer," he continued. "There's just nobody to get. Most of the fellows who made it back from the war stopped off somewhere else."

He put the bridle down. "I think Hans might be a really good man."

"The others?" Mama asked.

"A problem," Papa replied. "They're Germans who can't speak a word of English." He shook his head. "They're going to be three very lonely young men." He returned to the bridle. "The whole area is desperate for help. We'll just have to help them get jobs."

A chill went up Nina's spine at his words.

Suddenly she lifted her head. Going to the door, she looked cautiously toward the barn. In the twi-

light she could see the Germans. Carl played a har-
monica. Albert's fingers raced across the keys of
an accordion. Hans clapped and danced in time to
the music.

In spite of herself, Nina's feet began to move. "It
sounds just like a party," she said. Just then Hans
looked up and saw her in the doorway. For a
moment Nina's heart raced with fear, and she
fought the urge to run back inside. Then the
young German's face lit up with a smile, and Nina
felt herself smiling back. "They like to have fun
just like me," Nina said as she relaxed against the
doorway, her feet still tapping to the sound of the
music.

Vanished!

By Jenny Alloway

Fourteen-year-old Ben and his ten-year-old brother, Christopher, looked across the ship's broad deck at Governor John White. The artist and explorer spread his feet wide to avoid being tossed off balance by the roiling waves.

Christopher nudged his brother. "Go ahead, Ben, ask him."

Ben swallowed hard and approached the famous explorer. "Uh, . . . excuse me, sir," Ben said. "I hope I'm not disturbing you, sir."

Governor White looked at Ben. "I'm just whiling away the hours until we finally reach land, young man. I'm anxious to set my feet on dry, unmoving ground again. I guess you are, too."

"Yes, sir, I'll sleep sounder in a hammock that doesn't dump me out when the sea gets rough."

Governor White chuckled. "I'll never forget my first trip to the New World," he remembered. "It's a land of freedom and plenty for the person who isn't afraid of hard work."

"My brother and I plan to stay in the New World," Ben said, glancing across the ship at Christopher. "We thought we might settle in your colony on Roanoke Island."

Governor White smiled. "Well, you'll be welcome. We'll need all the willing hands we can get to carve a home out of the wilderness."

"When did the Roanoke Island Colony start?" Ben asked.

"I brought settlers here in 1587, but I had to go back to England for supplies. Then the war with Spain held me there for two years. Now I'm anxious to return. I left family there. My little granddaughter, Virginia Dare, was the first English child born in the New World." Governor White smiled at the thought.

"Ben, I believe I gave you work to do!" the ship's

captain barked, glaring down from the pilot's deck.

"Aye, Captain," Ben answered sheepishly.

"I look forward to having you and your brother join our Roanoke Island Colony," Governor White called after him as he scurried to do his chores.

Some days later, a sailor called out, "Land Ho, Captain, straight over the forward bow!"

Ben and Christopher craned their necks and searched the horizon. They saw a shadowy line floating above the ocean waves. Land! The dangerous voyage was almost over. Joining the weary crew, they cheered their arrival in the New World.

When the ship was safely anchored in a small cove, sailors busily transferred huge crates onto the top deck. Ben and Christopher perched atop the rail, impatient to get to land.

"You've finished your work, boys," the captain finally said.

"There's a path to follow," Mr. White added. "Let the folks at the colony know we've finally arrived."

The boys tied their shoes onto their belts and balanced on the rail. They lifted their arms and dove. Salt spray covered their heads and partially filled their mouths.

"Race you!" Ben sputtered.

Weighed down by heavy homespun breeches, the boys struggled toward the beach. Their feet soon sank deep into the sun-warmed sand.

"I don't see a path," Christopher said, as he knelt to buckle his shoes.

"Follow me," Ben replied, forcing his way into the thick underbrush. "Governor White said the colony was nearby. We'll find it."

Branches slapped their wet backs as they hiked deeper into the dark forest. The sun was covered by the thick trees above. Ben jumped when a rabbit sprang across his path. The grass grew taller than Christopher's head and folded around them like a green curtain.

"I hope we aren't lost," Christopher whispered fearfully. "I sure don't want to meet up with any wild animals."

"Don't worry," Ben replied. "The colony must be just up ahead."

Ben glanced over his shoulder at Christopher. Despite his reassurance, a sense of dread crept up his spine. Ben doubted his decision to bring his young brother to this wild place, where shadows took on the form of giant bears and phantom wolves peered from behind towering trees.

"Watch out!" Christopher cried, as Ben stumbled over a root snaking across the uneven ground.

With relief, Ben finally spied a rooftop through the trees. He hurried toward it with Christopher at his heels. They reached a log cabin but were disappointed to find it empty. The plank door sagged open on one rusty hinge.

The boys continued toward a larger clearing. They found more deserted buildings. No one rushed out to greet them.

Puzzled, Christopher asked, "Where is everyone?"

Ben shook his head and cautiously walked around the circle of log cabins, which were crumbling from lack of care. Holes gaped in the thatched roofs. The abandoned settlement stared back at them with blank windows like unblinking eyes.

"Ben, look here," Christopher called. "Look on this tree. Someone wrote a message here."

Ben moved closer to read the letters carved into the bark of the tree. **C R + A T**, he read. "I don't know what it means," Ben said, shaking his head.

Christopher called to the sailors as they entered the clearing. "Everyone's disappeared!"

Governor White studied the letters carved on the tree, **C R + A T**. His face showed the shock of finding the colony abandoned.

"Something very strange has happened here," he said in a worried tone. "It seems someone tried to leave us a clue."

"Did the Croatian Indians kidnap everyone?" Ben asked.

"I just don't know," Governor White replied. "There were friendly Croats in this area when I was last here. Maybe the people were starving and moved to live with them."

For weeks, Ben and Christopher joined in the attempt to solve the mystery. Traveling north along the Virginia coast, their party met a group of Englishmen. They learned nothing about the missing settlers from the Roanoke Island Colony, but their confidence grew as they became more familiar with the fertile hills and valleys of the New World.

Returning to camp one evening, Governor White sighed, saying, "Men, our search is useless. The people have simply vanished, leaving only one clue that we can't understand."

Ben felt sad for the great man who'd lost his daughter and granddaughter, as well as his dreams of governing a prosperous colony in the untamed New World.

"Ben, I guess you and Christopher will return to England with the ship," Governor White said. "You won't want to stay in this dangerous land now."

"Yes, we will," Christopher cried, hopefully.

Ben hesitated, thinking of the lost settlers. He also thought of the wonders he'd discovered: rich land for growing crops, plentiful wildlife for hunting, and streams of fresh water churning with fish.

How unlike the busy, crowded city he'd left behind in England!

Christopher looked at Ben, waiting for his reply.

"I reckon we'll be staying here, sir. Christopher and I came to begin a new life in this new land. More people are coming out every year now. I figure someday this will be a great nation."

"A great nation begins with brave lads like you and Christopher," Governor White said. "I think you'll survive the dangers and do well here."

"Yes, sir, I think we will," Ben replied.

THE SOD HOUSE

By June Swanson

Emma tugged at the block of sod her father had just cut. It was too heavy for her to lift. *If only I were bigger,* she thought, *or stronger like John and Joshua.* She sadly watched her brothers each pick up a block of sod, their muscles straining and tightening across their shoulders.

"Can I help, Pa?" she asked. "I want to help build our new house." Her father looked up. "Nothing you can do here, Emma. Ask Ma if she needs you."

Emma ran to where her mother was helping

the boys set the blocks in place to make the walls of the house. She remembered the instructions their neighbor, Mr. Ketchum, had given them for building a sod house. "You can't leave any cracks between the blocks of sod," Mr. Ketchum had said, "or the snakes and mice will get in." Emma shuddered. She hoped Ma was watching the boys carefully.

"Can I help you, Ma?" Emma asked.

Her mother straightened up and pushed the hair back from her face. Her hands were black with soil, and there was a dark smudge on the skirt of her gingham dress. "I don't think so, honey. You just brought us water from the spring. That was a big help."

"But I want to do something to help build the house," insisted Emma.

Her mother sighed. "This work is just too hard and too heavy for you. Why don't you go over by the wagon and play?"

As Emma turned away, she almost bumped into Joshua, who was struggling with a large piece of sod.

"Can I help you carry that?" she asked.

"No," Joshua grunted, "just get out of the way so I can put it down!"

Emma kicked little puffs of dust in front of her,

as she slowly walked toward the wagon. *There must be something I can do,* she thought. *Joshua and John will always be bragging that it's their house because they helped build it. And I won't have done anything!*

She slumped down beside the wagon and opened the wooden box Grandpa Reynolds had made for her. "Made this from Virginia pine," Grampa had said, "so you'll always have a part of Virginia with you." Emma lifted her old doll, Annie, out of the box and held her tightly.

Suddenly Emma felt very homesick. She wished she were back in Virginia sitting under a shade tree. There were only two trees on their whole claim here on the prairie—the two cottonwoods down by the spring. One hundred sixty acres and only two trees! Of course that's why they had to build the sod house. There were no trees for wood. Pa couldn't even find enough wood to stake off their claim. Instead he had piled up a stack of buffalo skulls on each corner of their land.

Emma watched Pa now as his plow cut the prairie into long strips. After each row he stopped and cut the strips into smaller blocks with his sharp ax. Emma sighed. Everybody was busy, and all she could do was sit and watch.

One by one Emma lifted the other things out of

her pine box. There was the apron Aunt Clara had made for her and the material Grandma Reynolds gave her for a new dress next winter. Emma rubbed her hand over the smooth pine box. She was glad she would always have this part of Virginia.

Emma shivered and looked up as a cloud passed over the sun. The sun was setting across the prairie, and it was beginning to cool off. Ma and Pa and the boys came toward her. Pa was talking to the boys and pointing to the boxes behind her. "Tomorrow we'll put in the door. I figure to take apart those two packing boxes we brought the tools and seed in to make the door and the frame. I had hoped to make a window frame or two, but I measured this morning and it doesn't look like there will be enough wood."

"Oh no," Ma cried, "we have to have some windows or it will be too dark inside. We need a window in the kitchen, at least."

"And one on the other side of the house," said Joshua, "to let a breeze blow through."

"I know," Pa answered tiredly, "but there just isn't enough wood."

"Could I take the wagon to Grand Island and buy some?" asked John.

"I'll go along and help," Emma added eagerly.

"No." Pa shook his head slowly. "Wood is too expensive in Nebraska. We just don't have the money."

Emma hugged Annie even tighter. *Maybe a sod house wasn't going to be very good after all,* she thought, *if it's dark and stuffy inside.*

"I wish there was a way," said Pa, "but I measured and figured every way I could and there just isn't enough wood for a door and windows too."

John nodded toward the two cottonwoods by the spring. "Could . . ." he began, but his father stopped him.

"No, son. We can't cut those. They may start seedlings, and then someday we'll have a lot more trees."

"Guess we should have brought some wood with us from Virginia," said Ma.

"Probably should have," agreed Pa, "but we didn't know there were so few trees in Nebraska and that lumber would be so expensive."

"Pa," Emma almost whispered, "I did bring some wood from Virginia. I brought the pine box Grandpa Reynolds made me. Is that enough for window frames?"

Pa looked thoughtfully at the box. "Yes, it would be, but we can't use it. It's your special box —your part of Virginia."

"But it would still be a part of Virginia even if it's made into windows," argued Emma. "Then our house would be part from Nebraska and part from Virginia—just like us! Please use it, Pa."

He looked at Ma. She nodded slightly and smiled. "Okay, Emma, if you're sure you want us to," Pa said.

"Oh, yes, I do!" Emma jumped up and laughed. "See, I knew I could help!"

AROUND THE HORN

By Virginia Germain

December 15, 1852

I, Edward Newmark, have just celebrated my twelfth birthday while sailing with my mother, sisters, and brother on this 140-foot, three-masted schooner, the *Carrington*. We are two days out of New York City, bound for San Francisco. It's a distance of 16,000 miles around Cape Horn, the tip of South America. We plan to meet my father in San Francisco. He left last year to open a general store for the miners who stayed there after the Gold Rush.

Last night thunder, lightning, and mountainous waves made the ship buck like a wild horse! The ship shot up each wave, then dropped, looping and banking as it shuddered from the slap of the waves ahead.

I huddled in my bunk under a damp blanket. My sister Matilda was shaking and crying as water poured into the cabin. I must admit, I was scared, too, when I saw the water carry off our stove pipe, fresh supplies, and our live Christmas turkey.

I must have fallen asleep, for I awoke to quiet and calm.

"The storm is finally over, but I don't want anyone on deck. It will take at least a day to dry out," Captain French announced. Stuck in our salt-water-soaked quarters for a day!

December 16, 1852

Today I climbed the rope ladder to the top deck. I saw sails and clothes drying in the breeze.

"Edward, I see you finally have your sea legs," the captain said. He actually spoke to me! I asked him what *sea legs* were, and he said that means you are used to the motion of the ship.

The rest of the day wasn't nearly as exciting. Mother sewed clothes for the family and took care of baby Harriet, who is just learning to walk. I had to keep an eye on my younger brother, Meyer.

Mother is a tiny woman with snappy black eyes and a busy, bustling manner. When she wants something done, her eyes take on a commanding look, and we mind immediately.

Matilda is my favorite sister; she always thinks of adventurous things to do. I think she would climb the rigging to the lookout if it were proper! Instead, we spend a lot of time playing drafts, a game like checkers.

December 25, 1852

Today everyone was out on deck looking at the sky, which was flashing with fireworks like the Fourth of July. Even without the turkey, we ate a fine holiday meal of roast chicken, plum pudding, vegetables, applesauce, and cider.

Miss French, the captain's daughter, played Christmas songs on the pianoforte. We are Jewish and don't usually celebrate Christmas. But since the other passengers and crew were singing Christmas songs, we spent most of the night enjoying the music.

My mother always lit candles on Friday night to bless the Sabbath at home in New York. The captain, his daughter, and the other passengers have told us that they look forward to listening to us recite the Sabbath prayers. It makes Mother happy when they tell her this.

January 12, 1853

I am reading *David Copperfield*. I turn the pages slowly and reread parts so that I have something more to do each day. When the ship rocks up and down in rough weather, I try to keep my mind on the story. The ocean around us seems endless on all sides.

February 1, 1853

Matilda was the first one to spy a ship today, and the captain gave her an orange. The ship was an American whaler that signaled and lowered a boat. They gave us sacks of vegetables and late newspapers. One sailor even gave Matilda a huge whale's tooth. They took Mother's letter for Grandma back to New York. One sailor taught me how to tie strong knots, and I've been practicing all day.

February 14, 1853

As we near Cape Horn, the weather grows worse. "Why are you dropping those weights over the side of the ship?" I asked the captain.

"We are checking the water depth so that we don't run into the rocks on shore," he told me.

February 18, 1853

Another storm hit last evening. The ship rocked violently. Some barrels broke loose and rolled on the deck, roaring with the sea like a huge drum to the music of crackling sheets of lightning. We saw several battered ships on the rocks. I'll certainly feel better when we round the Cape.

February 25, 1853

The strangest thing happened today. Two monstrous birds landed on the deck, and we caught them with a net. A sailor measured the wings of one, and they were thirteen feet long! I had never been so close to such a huge bird. Captain French told us the meat of the albatross looks like beef, but it isn't good to eat.

March 21, 1853

We sailed up the Pacific coast as the crew cleaned the decks, polished the brass bells and railings until they glowed, and set new sails. Thank goodness the weather has been nice lately. No more storms!

April 20, 1853

I heard the captain shout, "PORT" about 2 A.M. We were in San Francisco after four months!

At 10 A.M., Father came out to meet the ship. We said our goodbyes to Captain French and the crew and stepped on land. I still felt the motion of the ship! As my sea legs become land legs, I sense that ahead of me is a whole new life. I think, though, I'm going to miss the sailors, Captain French, and the thrill of riding the waves in a sturdy ship.

Sybil Ludington's Ride for Freedom

By Bonnie Highsmith Taylor

Sybil Ludington and her sister Rebecca were doing the supper dishes while their mother and sister Mary got the three youngest children ready for bed. Archie and Henry bickered as they carried in wood to fill the huge wood box.

"I carry twice as much wood as you do," nine-year-old Archie complained.

"Do not," countered eight-year-old Henry.

"Do too," snapped Archie. "I hate carrying wood. Girls don't have to. Girls have easy chores."

Sybil turned on him. "That's what you think, smarty. I'd trade places with you any day." She sighed. "If I were a boy, I'd be a colonial soldier in Papa's regiment."

"Oh, Sybil!" exclaimed Rebecca. "How could you want to be a boy?"

"Because boys fight in the war against the British, that's why. It's time those Red Coats were sent back where they belong. Then the colonies would be free and independent—"

She stopped as hoofbeats sounded in the distance. She ran to the door and looked out. A rider was coming toward the Ludington farm.

"Someone must be delivering a message to Papa," said Rebecca.

Their father, Henry Ludington, was a colonel in the Seventh Militia of Dutchess County, New York, so they were used to messengers arriving at all hours of the day and night.

The rider came to a halt in the yard and nearly fell from his horse. The poor beast was covered with lather, and the rider was caked with mud. Sybil knew the message must be important.

Papa came running from the barn and helped the weary traveler into the house. Archie yelled, "Henry, help me take care of his horse."

After drinking three dippers of water, the man

panted, "The—the British landed at Fairfield yesterday and marched into Danbury. They've set the town on fire. General Washington and his troops are in Peekskill. It would take days for them to get here."

Mr. Ludington said, "We need to get word to my men. They're scattered all over." He ran his fingers through his hair. "Someone will have to let them know to meet here so we can be ready to march at dawn."

"I'll go, Papa!" cried Sybil. "I know where all the soldiers live. I'll ride Star. He's the fastest horse in the whole world."

The young messenger stared at her. "You!" he exclaimed. "A girl! This is a man's job!"

Sybil fumed. Angrily she said, "I'm sixteen years old, I'll have you know. And I can ride as well as any man."

Colonel Ludington smiled at the shocked young man. "I believe she can, at that," he said, winking at his daughter.

He said, "I wouldn't let you go if I didn't have faith in you. I know you can handle Star even better than I can."

"I'll be fine, Papa," Sybil answered.

"I must be here to give orders to my men when they report for duty," Mr. Ludington said. "This man is too worn out." He gave Sybil a quick hug. "Be careful, Daughter."

Sybil wrapped her heavy cape over her head and shoulders. Before she went out the door, she turned to the messenger and said, "I'm sorry I was rude, sir, but this is not a job for a man. It's a job for a patriot."

As Sybil had claimed, Star was a very fast horse. Before she realized it, they had reached the first farmhouse. Sybil's voice rang out strong in the night air. "The British have burned Danbury! Sound the alarm, then meet at Ludington's at once!"

On she rode toward Shaw's Pond. "Good boy, Star," she whispered into the horse's ear. "You're a good soldier."

She stopped at three more farmhouses, calling out the message. Then she reached the dense, wooded area she would have to ride through to get to Red Mills.

Star's breathing was getting heavier. He stumbled and nearly fell. Sybil held on tightly. "It's all right, boy. Good Star."

Shadows seemed to close in all around her as they entered the forest. "I'm all alone," she whispered. "So all alone."

Then suddenly she heard hoofbeats on the path ahead. Quickly she slid out of the saddle and led

Star into a thicket. She held her breath until she thought her lungs would burst.

The riders drew close. As the moonlight fell on them, Sybil saw that they were six Red Coats. She froze. *Oh, please, Star,* she prayed silently, *don't move. Don't make a sound.*

After what seemed like hours, the Red Coats were gone. Sybil was soon riding hard again, past Red Mills, then toward Stormville.

Her body ached. The cold wind stung her face, and she no longer felt the reins in her numb fingers. Star's coat was wet with foamy sweat.

At every house where soldiers were sleeping, Sybil called out, "Danbury is burning! Meet at Ludington's and prepare to march! Tell everyone!"

Twice more Star's feet almost went out from under him. Sybil's eyes filled with tears, but there could be no rest for either of them yet.

"Poor boy," she murmured. "Poor brave boy."

She rode on and on through the dark night, calling out the message.

Dawn was breaking when at last Sybil and Star returned to the Ludington dooryard. More than four hundred colonial soldiers were gathered there, ready to march on the British.

Sybil's father helped her down from the limping, mud-caked horse. "What a brave girl my daughter is," he said proudly.

"Star was brave too," answered Sybil. "I must put her in the barn and rub her down."

Later, Sybil sat across the table from her sister Rebecca. Before them was a huge breakfast of eggs, bread, ham, and strong coffee.

"You were awfully brave," said Rebecca. "I'm so proud of you."

Sybil smiled at her sister, then let out a huge yawn.

"What was it like, Sybil?" asked Rebecca. "All alone in the middle of the night with Red Coats maybe nearby?"

Sybil shrugged her shoulders. "Well—I admit I was a little frightened," she said. "But no more than any soldier would have been."

The Girl
in the
Cracked Mirror

By John Hayes

Victoria's blue eyes gazed sadly at the piles of trunks, old furniture, and papers strewn about the floor of the attic. Late-afternoon rain splattered on the small glass window above her head. She picked up one of the papers and saw it was a page from one of Mama's old calendars, June 1886. Victoria's eyes welled with tears as she remembered what happened in that month last summer. Papa's accident, then his funeral. After that, she and Mama selling all their possessions and moving in with

Grandmere in her old house in Brooklyn, New York. She dropped the paper with a sob. *I miss him so,* she thought.

Mama's voice drifted up the attic stairs. "It's almost dinnertime." Sighing, Victoria stood up and walked to a large, full-length mirror that leaned against a stack of boxes. Victoria peered into it, shaking the dust from her long, velvet skirt and picking the cobwebs from her hair. The old mirror was yellow and cracked, and she was careful not to step on the few jagged pieces that were lying on the floor.

Suddenly Victoria's mouth dropped open. A girl about her age was in the mirror, and it looked like she was trying to get out. But the missing pieces of the mirror kept a full image from forming, trapping the girl inside the mirror.

Stunned, Victoria asked, "Who are you?"

"I am called Mary," the image answered. "I used to live here. When I left I forgot my doll. Now I have come back for it, but I cannot seem to get through. Who might thee be?"

"Victoria." Victoria was still too surprised to say anything else, so she just stared at the image before her. The gaps in the mirror where the glass was missing made Mary look like a puzzle that was not quite put back together. Part of Mary's head and her left arm below the elbow weren't there. Her right thigh was gone, too, and her right calf and foot stood unconnected to her body. The cracks in the broken mirror etched into Mary's skin and appeared as creases and folds in her clothing.

Mary's outfit was unlike any Victoria had ever seen. Her dress was long and plain, made of coarse homespun cloth. Over it was tied a plain apron of creamy linen. Mary's head was covered with an odd-looking gathered cap, and her shoes were soft leather moccasins.

"I think I can help you get out of there," Victoria said. "I'll put the broken pieces of the mirror back in place."

She picked up two pieces from the floor in front of the mirror and found a third in a corner near an old, broken toy drum. Carefully she fitted them into the mirror. Mary's arm appeared, then the missing piece of her head and hair.

Mary tried to step forward, but the missing leg held her back. Sadly she shook her head. "I cannot seem to walk to thee," she said.

"Wait, I have an idea," Victoria exclaimed.

She hurried across the attic and rummaged in a dusty, lidless trunk filled with junk. Pulling a small tin lid from inside, she ran back to Mary. She fitted the tin into the mirror where Mary's leg should have been. A feeble image of the leg appeared.

"Now try!" Victoria said.

Slowly Mary stepped forward through the mirror. She was all in one piece, but she limped a little.

" 'Tis weak, but I can walk, Victoria," Mary said. "I wish I could stay and play with thee, but I can't. I must find my doll before I leave."

Victoria was bursting with questions for Mary. "Where are you from? How did you get in the mirror?" The words tumbled over one another in their rush to get out.

Mary smiled. "I was born in the year of our Lord 1776. My father built this house to celebrate The Declaration of Independence and my birth, both of which happened that year. I lived here until my death in June of 1786.

Victoria's face fell. "What happened?"

Mary patted Victoria's arm. "Do not fret. It was the smallpox, and I don't remember it. But I left behind my doll, and I get quite lonely without her."

Victoria took Mary's hand and said, "I know most everything here. What did your doll look like?"

"She is small, about the size of my hand," Mary said. "Her face is carved from wood, and she has black beads for eyes. Her hair is made from horsehair and hangs in two braids. Mother made her dress from old scraps of red wool. She was a gift from my parents, and she is very beautiful."

"I'd remember her," Victoria said. "I've never seen her."

The smile faded from Mary's face. Then Victoria got an idea. "Do you know of any secret hiding places?" she asked.

A grin formed on Mary's cracked features. "I know one."

She led Victoria to the back of the attic where the brick chimney rose through the floor and disappeared through the roof. "There's a hollow brick in the chimney," Mary said. She counted bricks for a moment, then grasped a brick and pulled it out. Eagerly she reached her pale hand into the small hole. "Nothing," she said sadly.

"We'll look everywhere," Victoria said.

They looked for hollow spaces by tapping the walls, they checked for loose floor boards, searched the rafters, and rummaged through boxes.

"Nothing," Victoria said finally. "Let's rest awhile." She turned toward Mary and accidentally kicked something hard. It rolled onto the middle of the floor.

"Bother," Victoria said.

"What's wrong?" Mary asked.

"This drum. It's in the way," Victoria replied.

"I remember that drum," Mary said. "My brother made the most terrible noise with it."

"It must have been fun when you lived here," Victoria said quietly.

"Yes, but there was a lot of work, too," Mary replied. She looked wistfully around the attic, remembering her life in the house so long ago. "I thank thee for all thy help, but I am afraid my doll is gone for good. I must leave now." A small tear trickled down Mary's cracked cheek.

"Will you come back?" Victoria pleaded. "It gets so lonesome in this house with no one but Mama and Grandmere to talk to."

"I do not know if I can," Mary said. She squeezed Victoria's hand in farewell and stepped into the mirror.

"At least I found a toy," Victoria said. "Would your brother mind if I fixed up his drum?" She picked up the faded toy and felt something move inside. She reached inside and felt the doll.

"Mary, wait! Your doll's inside the drum!" Victoria shouted. Mary turned at the sound of Victoria's cry, and her eyes lit when she saw her doll in Victoria's hand.

"Let me see her, please!" Mary said, stretching

her arms out of the mirror. Victoria handed her the doll, and Mary looked up at Victoria with a joyful smile. "She is just as I remembered."

"She is beautiful," Victoria agreed.

Mary drew her hands into the mirror, but they stopped when the doll touched the yellowed glass. "What's wrong?" Mary asked. She began to cry as she tried again to bring the doll into the mirror.

"The doll cannot go back with you." Victoria said. "She doesn't belong in the mirror."

With a sob, Mary dropped the doll on the attic floor and turned to go.

"Victoria, I'm fading. Care for the doll. She is yours now."

"I'll treasure it," Victoria answered. She clutched the tiny, fragile doll as she watched Mary vanish. Then she stooped and picked up the drum.

"I think I'll paint you blue and gold, with just a dab of red. Then I'll set my doll on top of you," she said.